TRUCKS!
(and other things with wheels)

First published in hardback in 2020
This paperback edition published in 2023 by Welbeck Children's Books
An imprint of Welbeck Children's Limited,
Part of the Welbeck Publishing Group
Offices in: London - 20 Mortimer Street, London W1T 3JW
Sydney - 205 Commonwealth Street, Surry Hills 2010
www.welbeckpublishing.com

Associate Publisher: Laura Knowles
Editor: Jenni Lazell
Design Manager: Emily Clarke
Designer: Dani Lurie

A CIP record for this book is available from the Library of Congress.

ISBN: 978 1 80453 589 9

Printed in Heshan, China

10 9 8 7 6 5 4 3 2 1

MIX
Paper | Supporting
responsible forestry
FSC® C020056

TRUCKS!
(and other things with wheels)

Written by
Bryony Davies

Illustrated by
Maria Brzozowska

This book belongs to:

Contents

Farm truck

Flatbed truck carrying pipes

Lugger truck

Monster trucks can do tricks and jumps. Their tires are much taller than you!

Tractor trailer

Garbage truck

Snowplow

Heavy-duty electric truck

Billboard truck

Military truck

Flatbed truck loaded with straw

Electric truck

Fuel truck

Dekotora trucks are from Japan. They are decorated from top to bottom with paint and neon lights.

Double-trailer truck

Car transporter

Trucks

Garbage trucks and mining trucks, transporter trucks and pickup trucks— trucks can be large or small, and take things where they need to go. Beep, beep!

Telescope antenna transporter

Pakistani jingle trucks are covered in bells and chains that jingle.

Christmas tree truck

Amphibious trucks can drive on land and also go in the water.

Mining truck

Rusty old pickup truck

Food truck

Milk truck

Recycling truck

Shiny new pickup truck

At the Gas Station

Different types of cars need different types of fuel.

The minivan is piled high with bikes and luggage. Where is it going?

1

2

This electric minicompact car is heading to a charging point.

There are many different vehicles here. Everybody needs to **fill up** with fuel before a long drive.

The car inside the car wash is getting squeaky clean!

Camper

Motor scooter

Check out these fun flowers! What design would you like on your car?

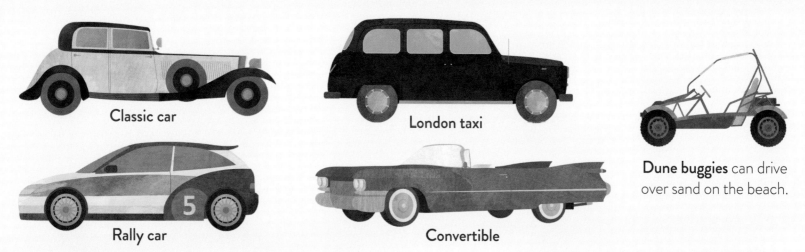

Classic car

London taxi

Rally car

Convertible

Dune buggies can drive over sand on the beach.

Cars, Vans, and Buses

Some cars are designed to go as fast as possible, while others are small for busy cities, or big and spacious for large families. Look at the different kinds of buses and taxis that carry passengers.

Camper van

Station wagon

SUV

This **Hot rod** has been painted with flames and given a powerful engine.

London double-decker bus

Hatchback

Super cars are very fast and extremely expensive.

Stretch limo

Minicompact car

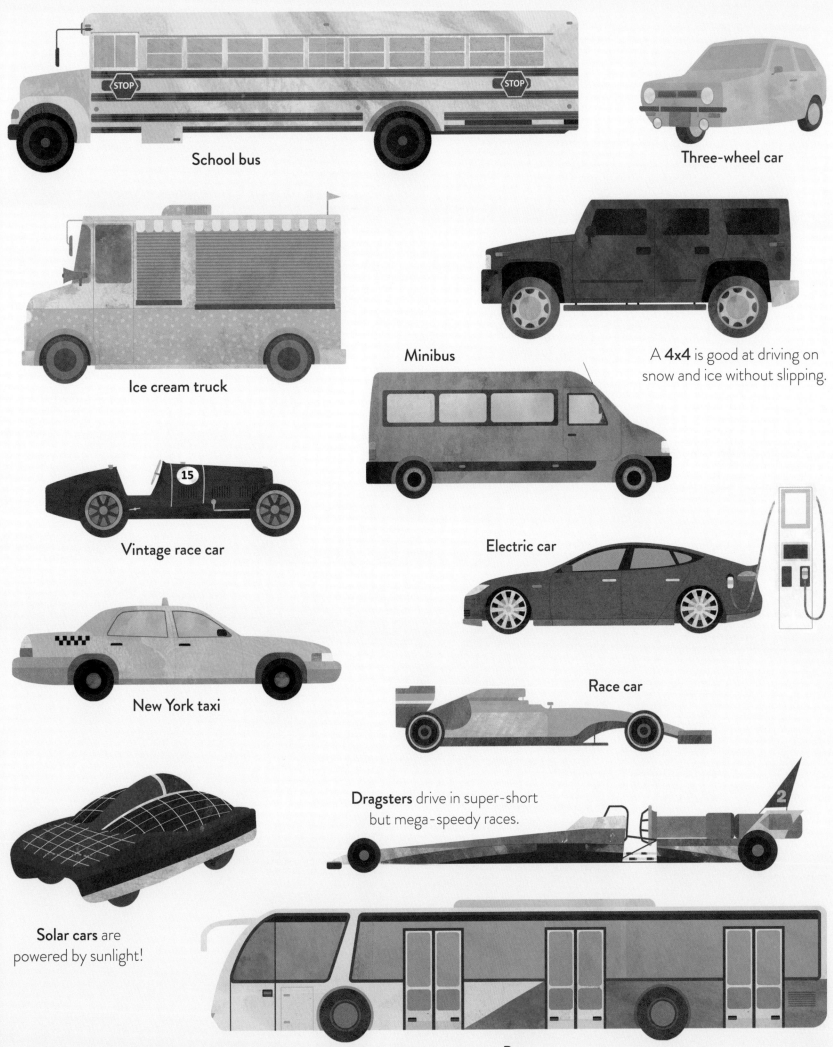

School bus

Three-wheel car

Ice cream truck

Minibus

A **4x4** is good at driving on snow and ice without slipping.

Vintage race car

Electric car

New York taxi

Race car

Dragsters drive in super-short but mega-speedy races.

Solar cars are powered by sunlight!

Bus

Let's Race!

Monster truck

Rally car

Vintage race car

Sports car

And they're off!
Which is your
favorite race car?

Go-kart

Highway Havoc

How many vehicles
with bicycles can
you spot?

Cars and trucks of all different shapes and sizes drive along the highway. Where are they all going? **Don't get stuck in traffic!**

Construction workers use a road roller to flatten new road.

At the Fire Station

A long ladder is extended to reach the fire.

Jets of water shoot out of the hoses to put out the flames!

These firefighters are practicing how to put out a fire in a tall building.

More firefighters bring ladders to reach the fire.

This fire engine is about to go to a real emergency! Turn on the flashing lights and sound the siren—it's time to go!

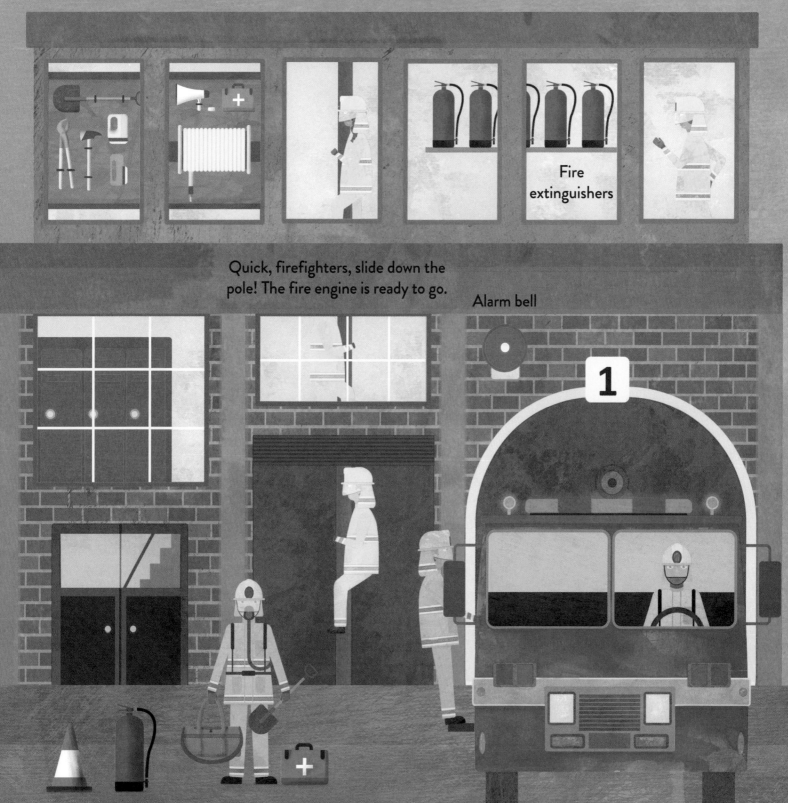

Fire extinguishers

Quick, firefighters, slide down the pole! The fire engine is ready to go.

Alarm bell

1

The firefighters gather all the things they will need to rescue people in danger.

Inside a Fire Engine

Deluge gun

Tools

Fire station dog

Pump panel

Helmet

Hose

Firefighters store all the equipment they need inside a fire engine. Everything has its proper place. What can you see?

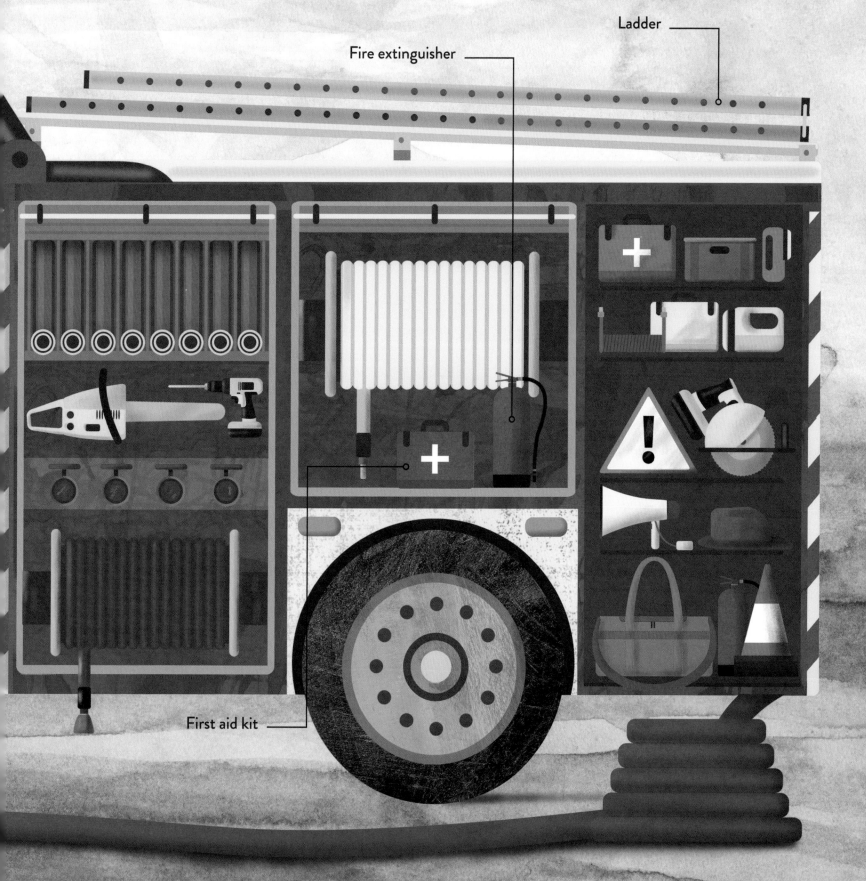

Ladder

Fire extinguisher

First aid kit

Emergency!

Would you rather be a firefighter in a shiny red truck,
a police officer with flashing lights, or a paramedic
rushing to help those who are sick or injured?

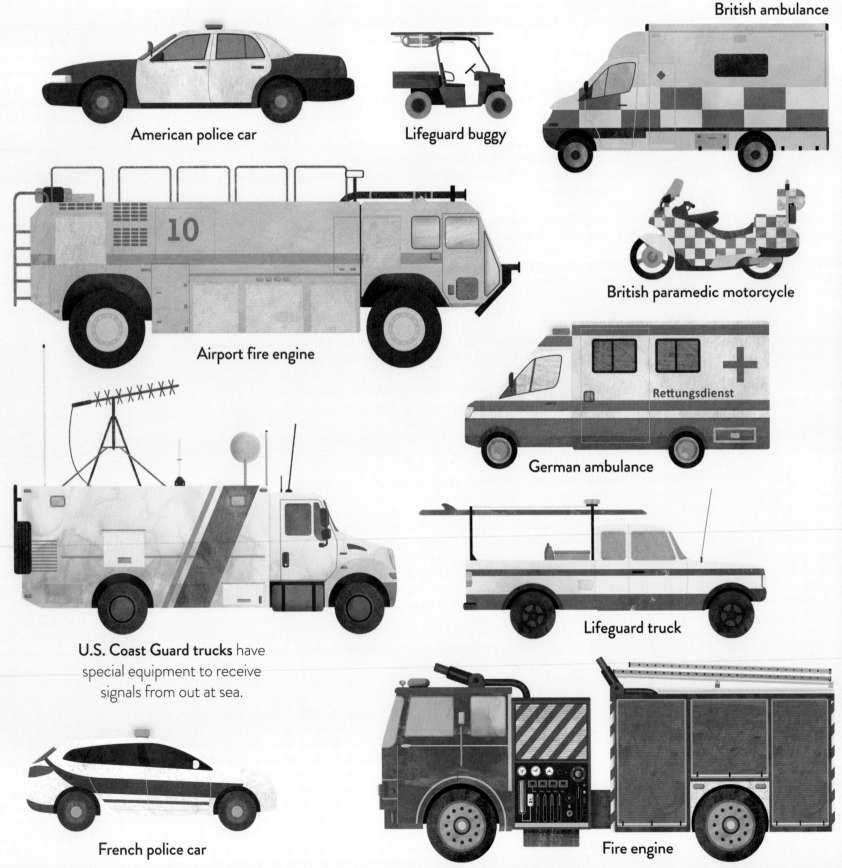

American police car

Lifeguard buggy

British ambulance

Airport fire engine

British paramedic motorcycle

German ambulance

Rettungsdienst

U.S. Coast Guard trucks have
special equipment to receive
signals from out at sea.

Lifeguard truck

French police car

Fire engine

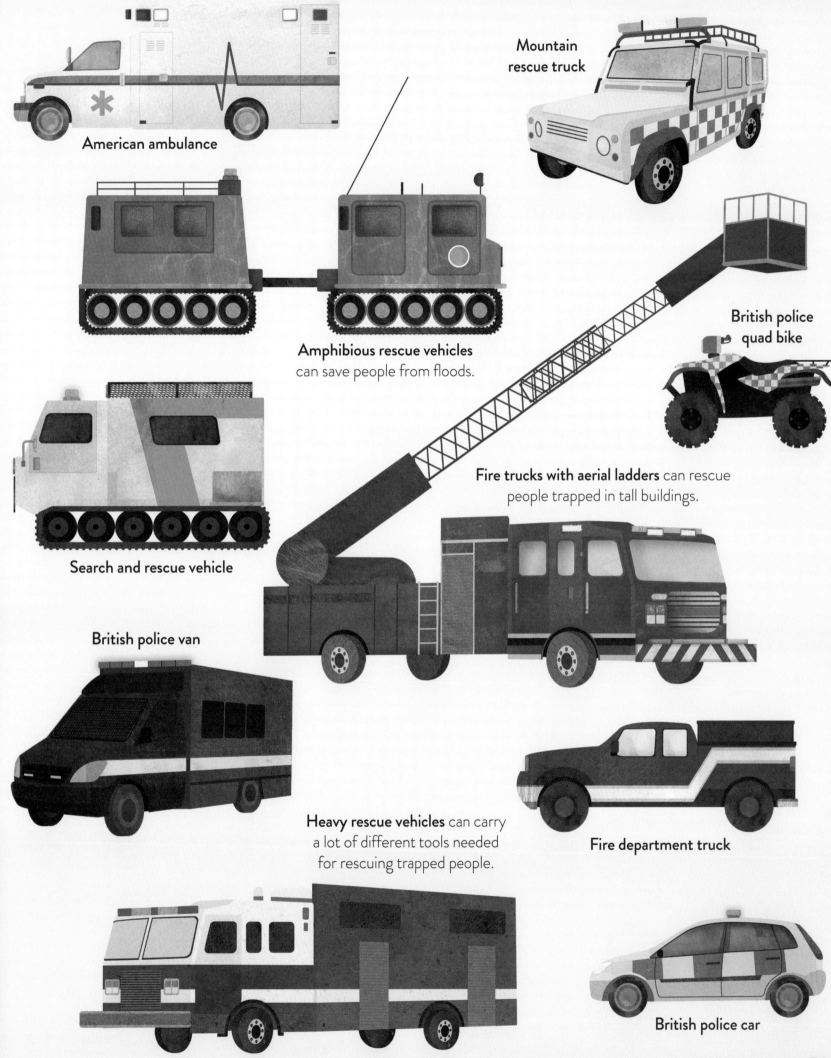

American ambulance

Mountain rescue truck

Amphibious rescue vehicles can save people from floods.

British police quad bike

Fire trucks with aerial ladders can rescue people trapped in tall buildings.

Search and rescue vehicle

British police van

Heavy rescue vehicles can carry a lot of different tools needed for rescuing trapped people.

Fire department truck

British police car

21

In the Old Days

12

Climb the stairs at the back of the bus to ride on the open top deck.

Have a look at this street scene from London more than a hundred years ago. Cars looked very different back then.

Instead of traffic lights, a traffic policeman tells cars when to go.

Car horn

Spare tire

Track bicycle

Electric bikes have a motor that helps you ride up hills.

Racing motorbike

You need good balance to ride a **unicycle**.

Stunt bike

Taxi bike

Tricycle

Child's bicycle

You can learn to do cool tricks on a **BMX**.

Bicycle with child's seat

Harley-Davidson engines are louder than a car!

Classic road bicycle

Motorcycle and sidecar

Road bicycle

Surrey bike

Awesome Bikes

Bikes can travel on roads, up mountains, and even on water! Would you like to ride one with one, two, or three wheels?

Electric scooter

Folding bicycle

Cargo bicycle

Rickshaw

Recumbent tricycle

Mountain bikes have bigger tires to ride over bumpy ground.

Snowbike

Tandem bicycle

Pedicab

Motor scooter

Classic bicycle

Water bike

25

Pedal Power

All these people are out for a bike ride. It's hard work going uphill, but lots of fun **whizzing back down!**

Unicycle

Pedicab

Tandem bicycle

Everyone wears a helmet to keep them safe if they fall off their bicycle.

BMX

Would you enjoy zooming down a steep hill?

Milk tanker

Cabless tractor

ATVs have thick tires to help them drive over soft or muddy ground.

Mini loader

Tracked tractor

Tractor with snowplow

On the Farm

Tractors and trucks have all kinds of jobs to do on the farm. Some carry animals, and others help plant and harvest crops. Which would you like to drive?

Tractor with bale loader

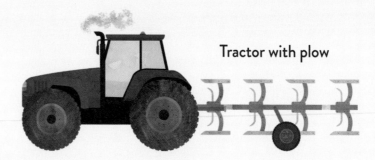

Tractor with plow

Combines have a ladder to help the drivers climb into the cab.

Skid steer loader

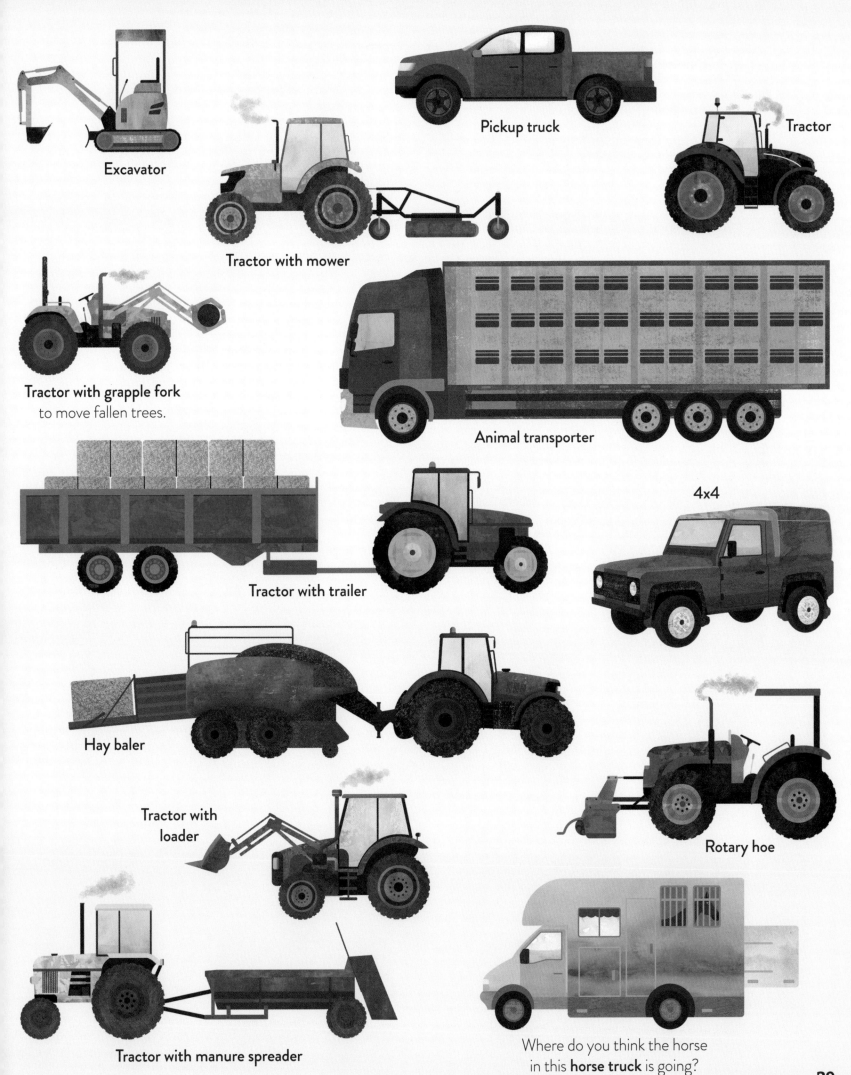

Excavator

Pickup truck

Tractor

Tractor with mower

Tractor with grapple fork
to move fallen trees.

Animal transporter

4x4

Tractor with trailer

Hay baler

Rotary hoe

Tractor with
loader

Tractor with manure spreader

Where do you think the horse
in this **horse truck** is going?

Inside an Ice Cream Truck

Can you hear that jingle? It's the ice cream truck!

Loudspeaker

Sprinkles

Sauces

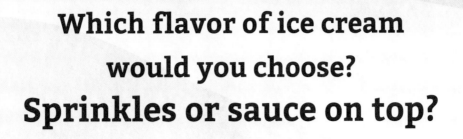

Which flavor of ice cream would you choose?
Sprinkles or sauce on top?

Refrigerator

Lollipops

Ice cream cones

Ice cream flavors

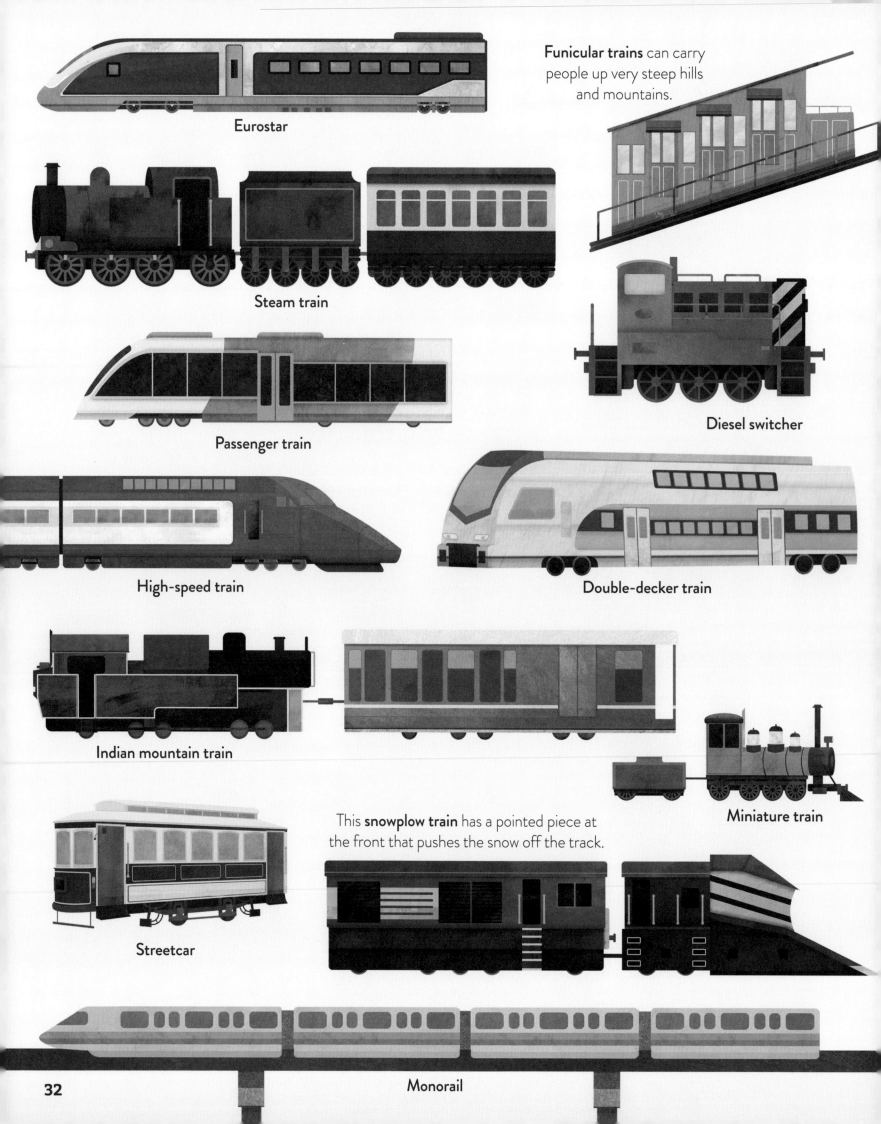

Eurostar

Steam train

Passenger train

High-speed train

Funicular trains can carry people up very steep hills and mountains.

Diesel switcher

Double-decker train

Indian mountain train

Miniature train

Streetcar

This **snowplow train** has a pointed piece at the front that pushes the snow off the track.

Monorail

Modern streetcar

Firefighting train

London Underground train

Trains

Trains run on tracks and can travel long distances without getting stuck in traffic. They can be powered by steam, diesel, or electricity.

High-speed steam locomotive

Diesel engine

French Metro train

Japanese bullet trains are super speedy! They are the fastest type of train.

Freight train

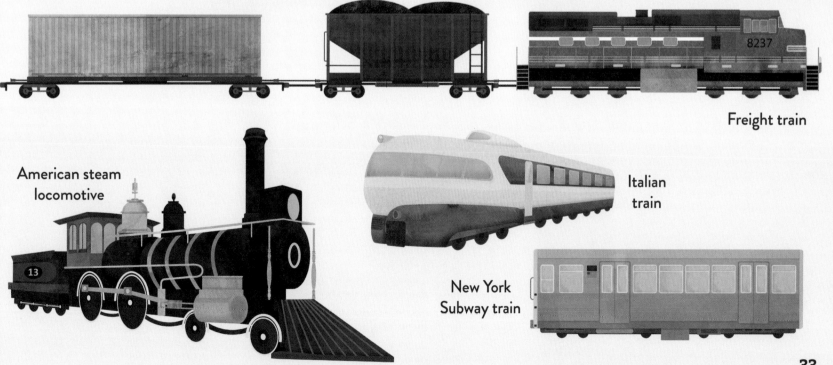

American steam locomotive

Italian train

New York Subway train

33

Construction Vehicles

These machines can build anything from long, flat roads to the tallest towers. Some have gigantic wheels, some have long arms to dig or push dirt, and some have trays to carry heavy loads. Look at all the amazing tools they use!

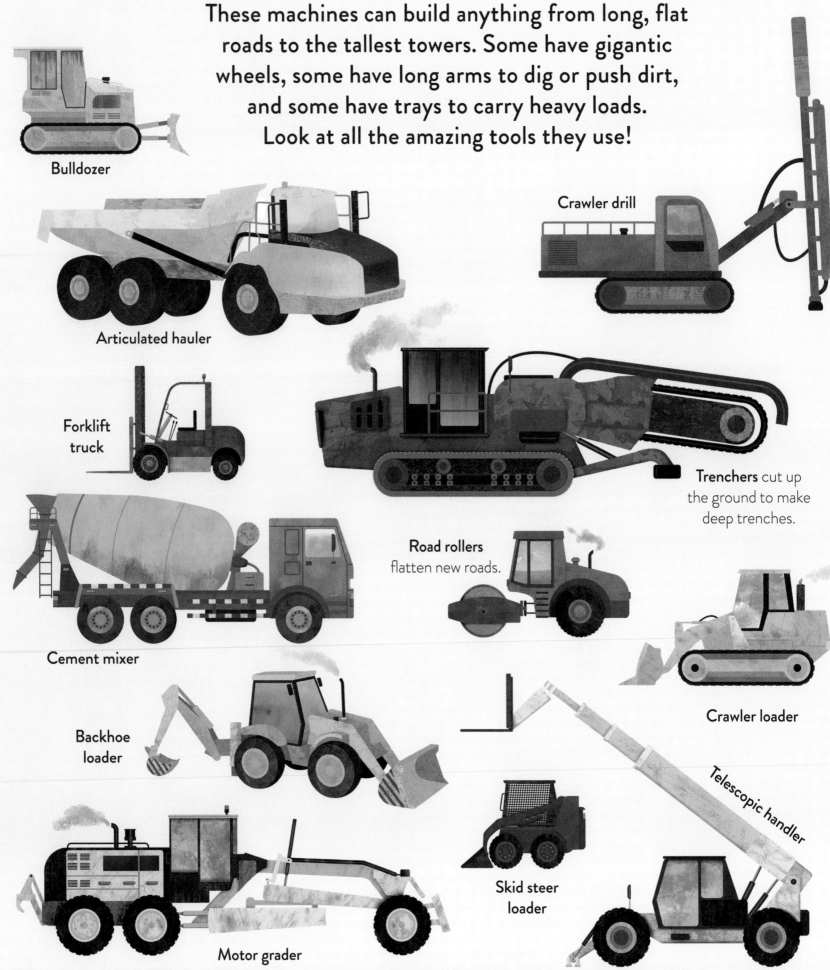

Bulldozer

Crawler drill

Articulated hauler

Forklift truck

Trenchers cut up the ground to make deep trenches.

Road rollers flatten new roads.

Cement mixer

Crawler loader

Backhoe loader

Telescopic handler

Skid steer loader

Motor grader

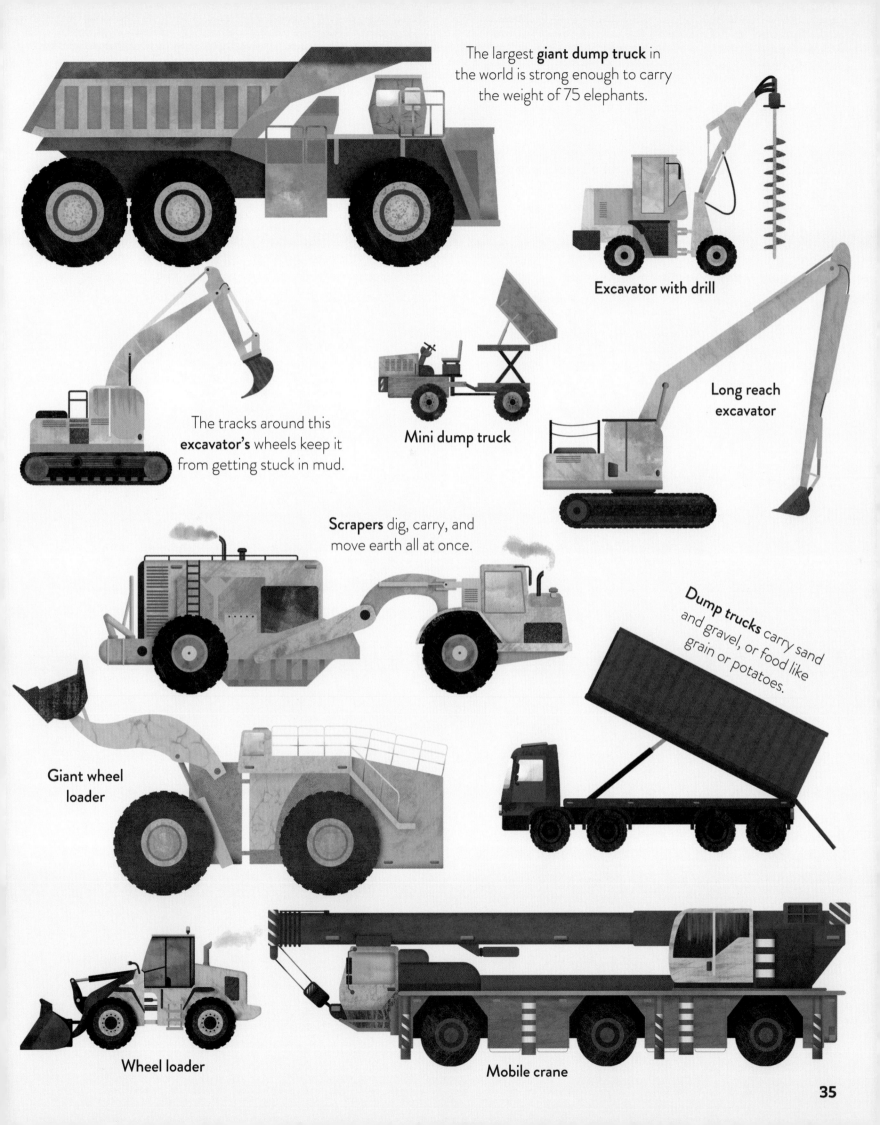

The largest **giant dump truck** in the world is strong enough to carry the weight of 75 elephants.

Excavator with drill

The tracks around this **excavator's** wheels keep it from getting stuck in mud.

Mini dump truck

Long reach excavator

Scrapers dig, carry, and move earth all at once.

Dump trucks carry sand and gravel, or food like grain or potatoes.

Giant wheel loader

Wheel loader

Mobile crane

Inside a Freight Train

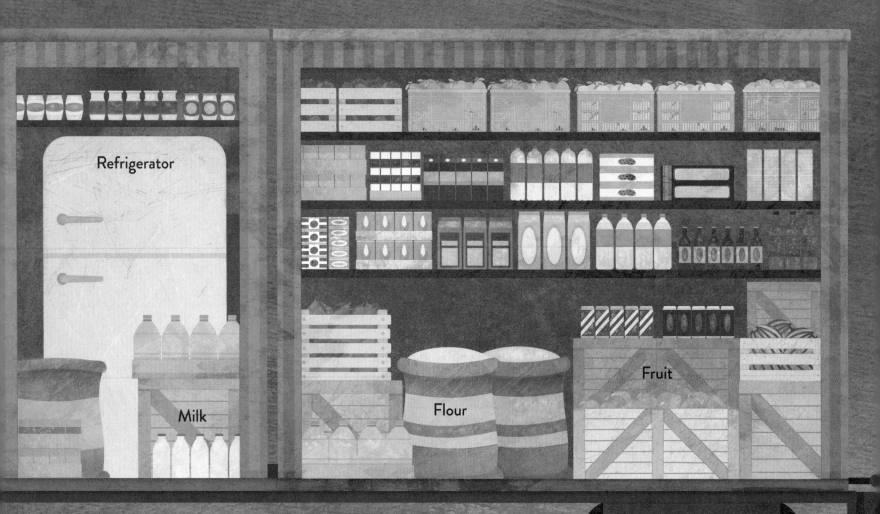

Freight trains can be hundreds of cars long!

Grain

8237

Refrigerator

Milk

Flour

Fruit

Freight trains are filled with all kinds of things. They travel long distances, carrying different cargo from place to place. What's inside this one?

Coal

Oil tank car

Cars

Tracks

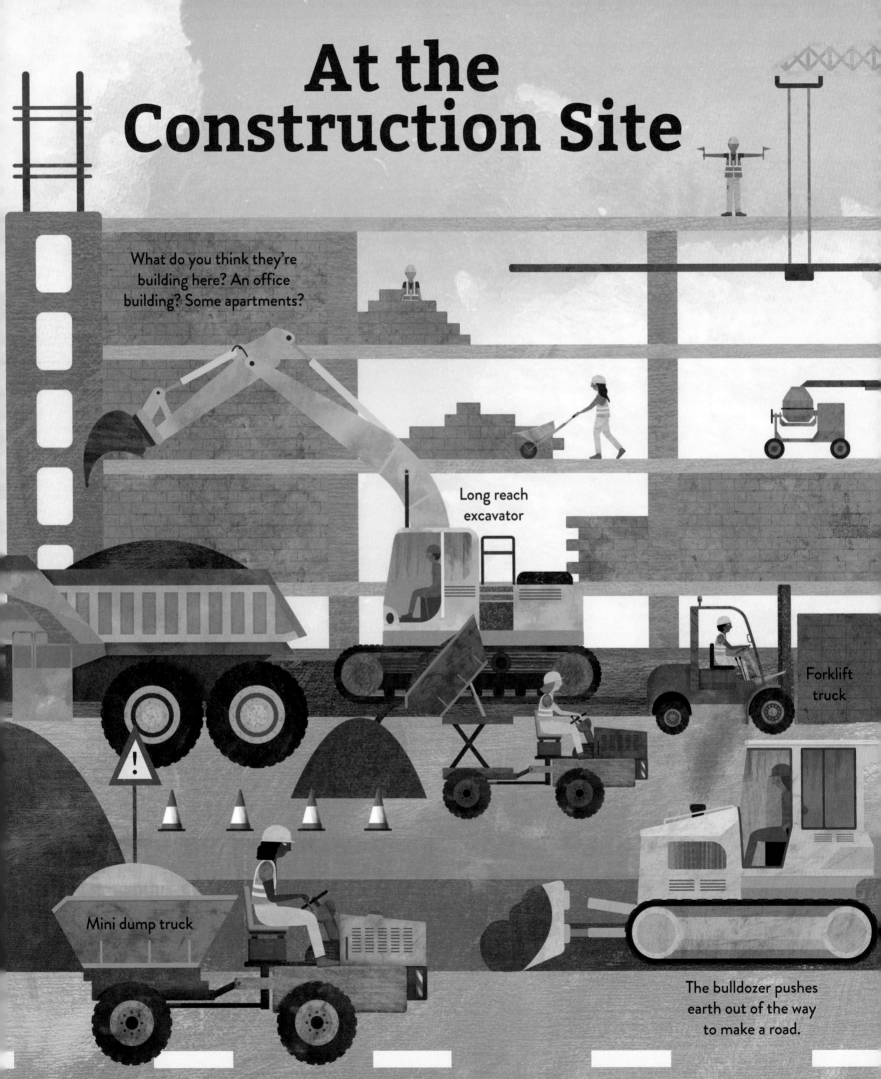

At the Construction Site

What do you think they're building here? An office building? Some apartments?

Long reach excavator

Forklift truck

Mini dump truck

The bulldozer pushes earth out of the way to make a road.

The machines are hard at work digging, dumping, and building things on the construction site. They all have to work together as a team to get the jobs done.

Crane

Cement mixer

This dump truck is unloading gravel.

Road roller

At the Airport

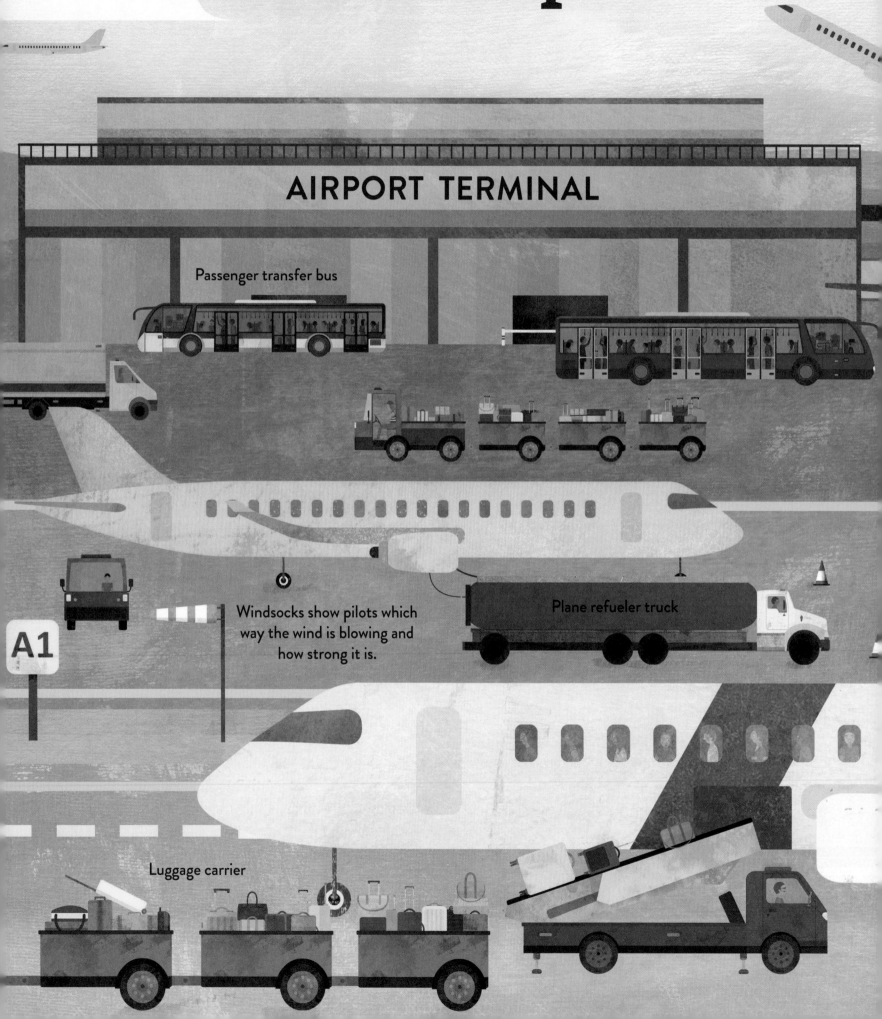

AIRPORT TERMINAL

Passenger transfer bus

Windsocks show pilots which way the wind is blowing and how strong it is.

A1

Plane refueler truck

Luggage carrier

It's very busy at the airport.
Trucks drive here and there,
making sure the planes are
ready for takeoff.

People in the air traffic
control tower tell the
planes when they can
take off and land.

Monorail

10

Airport fire engine

Passengers use aircraft
stairs to board the plane.

A2

This truck is unloading food for
the passengers on the plane.

Catering truck

At the Scrapyard

Vehicles are stacked on metal frames so mechanics can find parts that still work.

A long-armed machine picks up cars ready to crush them.

Old, used vehicles are brought to the scrapyard to be taken apart and recycled. It's full of car parts and tires.

These cars are crushed flat to make more space in the scrap yard.

Beep, beep! Watch out—this bulldozer is coming through!

Wheely Fun Facts

1. Monster trucks can do huge jumps. The longest ever monster truck jump was over 236 feet long. That's about the length of 15 cars!

2. The longest road train ever was almost one mile long. It would take you about 18 minutes to walk from one end to the other.

3. The highest backflip on a bicycle was nine feet high.

4. A car exists that's in the shape of a hotdog, and it's called the Wienermobile!

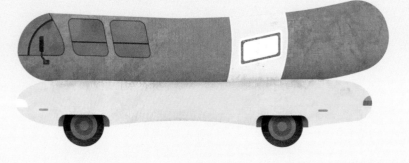

5. The fastest ever car is called Thrust SSC and it traveled at 763 miles per hour. That's about 10 times faster than a family car would drive on a highway.

6. The smallest car ever made is called the Peel P50. It only has one door and one headlight, and it can be picked up!

7. Excavators can dance! There is a group of huge excavators that can perform tricks, spins, and wave their buckets in the air to music.

8. Bagger 293 is an enormous bucket-wheel excavator. It uses buckets to scoop up earth and then drop it on conveyor belts to carry it away. Weighing in at 15,648 tons, it is the largest and heaviest land vehicle on Earth.

9. The longest passenger train is called The Ghan and it runs across Australia. It can have as many as 44 carriages and is over 2,526 feet long.

10. There's enough train track in India to circle Earth almost three times.

Can You Find?

Take a look through the book and see which of these items and vehicles you can find!

Trophy

Helmet

Electric scooter

Unicycle

Cement mixer

ATV

Ladder

Luggage truck

Ice cream sundae

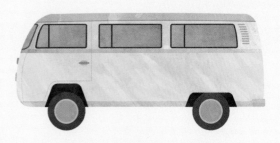

Camper

Tires

Christmas tree

Traffic policeman

Go-kart

Charging point

Mini dump truck

British paramedic motorcycle

Miniature train

Carwash

Fire station dog

Traffic cone
How many traffic cones can
you spot in the book?

Vrooom
vrooom!